PUSS IN BOOTS

Illustrated By
Johan Klingler & Norma Rivera
From The Tale By
Charles Perrault

The Unicorn Publishing House, Inc.
New Jersey

PUSS IN BOOTS

There was once a poor miller who died. Now this miller had three sons, and to them he left all that he owned. The sons divided the property among themselves. The oldest brother took the mill, the middle brother took the donkey, and the youngest brother was left with only the miller's cat.

The youngest brother was very unhappy with his poor share. He shook his head sadly, saying: "My two brothers shall be able to make a living with their shares, but I will only have a muff to keep me warm after I skin the cat."

The cat overheard the terrible fate awaiting him and decided to speak. "Young master, do not worry; if you will but give me a good strong sack, a pair of boots for my feet, and a hat to keep the sun from my face, you will soon see that *you* have been given the best share of your father's estate."

The young man didn't place any great hope on the cat's words, but he did remember how clever and cunning the cat could be in catching mice. So, with nothing much to lose, he *gave* the cat what he asked for.

Puss pulled on his boots, fit the hat snugly on his head, and slung the sack over his shoulder. And with a tip of his hat, he set off down the road; whistling a happy tune.

Puss set off to where he knew a great many rabbits were to be found. Placing a few carrots in the sack, he put it down in a clearing and then hid himself in the bushes.

No sooner had he hid than a group of fat rabbits came by and went straight into the sack. Puss *jumped* out from his hiding place and pulled the strings on the sack, trapping his catch.

Very pleased with himself, Puss threw the sack over his shoulder, and set off for the royal palace at once.

At the palace he asked to see the king. He was shown into the royal court, where he made a low bow and doffed his hat before the king.

"Your Majesty," Puss said, "please accept these fat rabbits as a gift from my master, the marquis of Carabas." (This was the name Puss had decided to call his young master.)

"Tell your master," the king replied, "that we thank him for his gift, which gives us *great* pleasure."

Puss once again gave a gracious bow, and then left.

The next day Puss went to a cornfield where a great many partridges gathered. He put a few kernels of corn inside the sack and then hid among the stalks. Before long four fat partridges ran right into the sack. Puss *pounced* and drew the sack shut. Then he was off once again to the royal palace.

Puss presented the partridges to the king, just as he had done with the rabbits. The king accepted them with equal pleasure and again bid Puss to thank the marquis of Carabas.

For two or three months Puss went on in this way, taking the king occasional presents of game or fish. Then one day he learned that the king was to take a drive along the riverbank with his daughter, who was as yet unmarried.

"Now," Puss said to his master, "if you do as I tell you, your fortune shall be made. All you have to do is go for a swim in the river at a spot I shall show you, and leave the rest to me."

The young man had no idea what good it would do him to take a swim in the river, but he did as his cat *told* him.

While he was swimming, the king came by, and Puss began to scream at the top of his voice, "Help, *help!* The marquis of Carabas is drowning!"

At these cries, the king put his head out of the coach window, and, recognizing the cat who had so often brought him gifts, ordered his guards to hurry to the rescue of the young man.

As they were pulling the young man from the river, Puss went up to the royal coach and told the king that as his master was bathing some thieves had come along and carried off his clothes. In truth, Puss had *hidden* them under a stone.

The king immediately commanded a man to return to the palace and fetch one of his best suits for the marquis of Carabas. Once the young man was dressed in the fine clothes of the king, he looked quite handsome, and the princess was taken with him at once. The king, seeing his daughter's fondness for the young man, invited him into the coach to continue the ride with them.

Puss, delighted to see his plan going so well, ran on ahead, and presently came upon some peasants mowing a fine lawn. "Listen well, good people," Puss called out to them; "unless you tell the king that the lawn you are cutting belongs to the marquis of Carabas, you will all be *chopped* into little pieces!"

And sure enough, the king asked the peasants whose fine lawn they were mowing.

"It belongs to the marquis of Carabas," they all answered together, terrified by Puss's threat.

"You have a fine estate," said the king to the marquis. The young man smiled graciously, but said nothing. He laughed inside, though, as he began to understand what his cat was up to. "That clever Puss!" he thought.

Puss went farther on ahead until he came upon some reapers cutting and rolling hay. "Listen well, good harvesters," Puss called out to them; "unless you tell the king that this hayfield belongs to the marquis of Carabas, you will all be *chopped* into little pieces!"

A moment later the king passed by and asked the reapers who owned the hayfield.

"The marquis of Carabas," they all answered.

"My word," the king said. "I congratulate you, sir, for your wealth must be great."

And still Puss ran ahead. At last he came to a splendid castle. It belonged to an ogre who was the richest ever seen. In fact, all the lands the king had passed were really part of his estates. Puss boldly walked in, knowing full well of the ogre's might and magic. And, of course, Puss had a plan.

The ogre received Puss as politely as an ogre can and asked why he had come to his castle. Puss stepped forward and gave a low bow, saying, "I have been told that you have the power to change yourself into any kind of animal—that you can, for instance, change into a lion, perhaps?"

"Quite true, cat," the ogre said gruffly; "and to show you, *behold the lion!*"

Puss almost jumped out of his boots, for in the next moment, a huge lion stood before him.

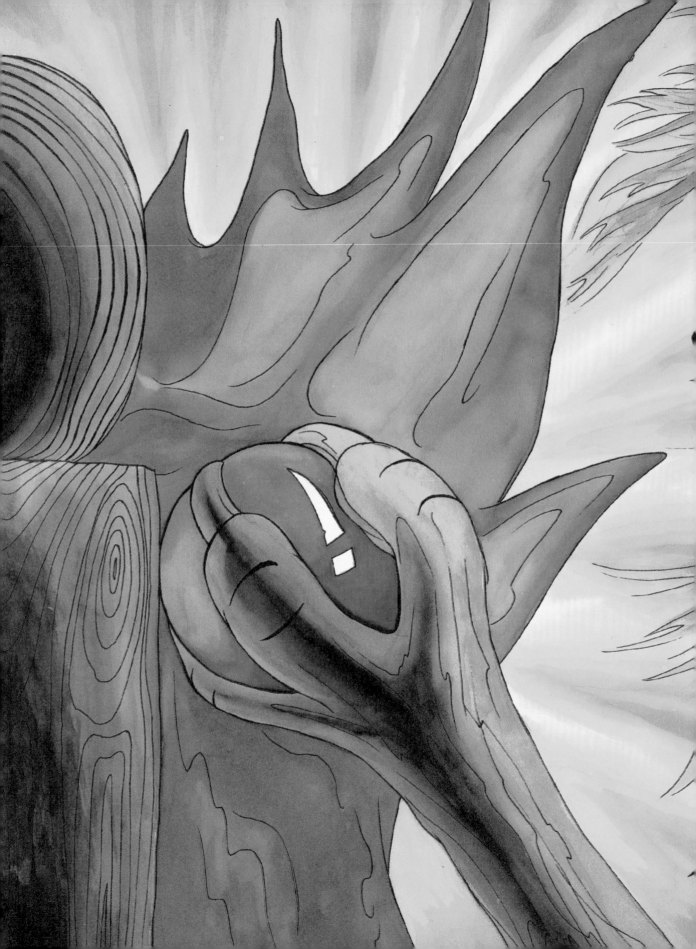

But Puss took courage and stepped up nose to nose with the lion. "Impressive, my lord," said Puss with just a little tremble in his voice; "but I have heard your magic is *even* greater, though I can scarcely believe it."

"What do you mean, cat!" roared the ogre.

"I have heard that you have the power to change into the smallest of animals as well," Puss said boldly. "For instance, to change into a mouse would *really* be something, though I think it would be quite impossible, even with your powers."

"Impossible!" the ogre roared. "Behold, stupid cat!"

Instantly he changed himself into a mouse and began to run about the floor. "Impressive, my lord, *really quite* impressive!" laughed Puss.

The ogre realized too late that he had been tricked. Puss pounced on the little mouse and ate him up.

After a while the king came by, and, seeing the ogre's splendid castle, was anxious to go inside.

Puss heard the carriage outside and ran out to meet the king.

"Welcome, Your Majesty," Puss cried out, "to the castle of the marquis of Carabas."

"The marquis!" exclaimed the king, "does this *fine* castle belong to him?"

"If it please, Your Majesty," said Puss; "let me show you my master's fine home." And they went inside the castle and feasted on the fine meal that the ogre had set out for himself.

The king was so delighted with the young man (as well as his vast wealth) that it wasn't long before the marquis of Carabas was wed to the beautiful princess. The marquis of Carabas and the princess moved into the castle and lived quite happily, I am told.

And what of Puss, *you* might ask?

Well, as for Puss, he became a very great lord indeed and gave up chasing mice. Except, of course, when it *amused* him—from time to time.

This book is dedicated
to Greg, Tim, Jean, Mary & Lou.
With Love.